My Family

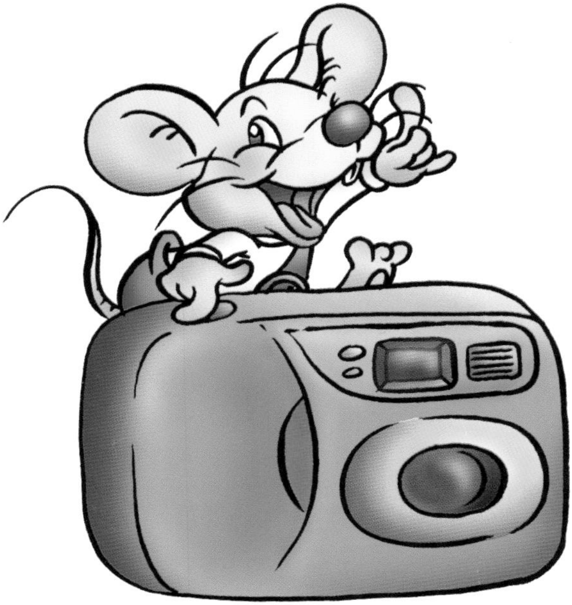

Illustrated by Stella Yang

Rigby

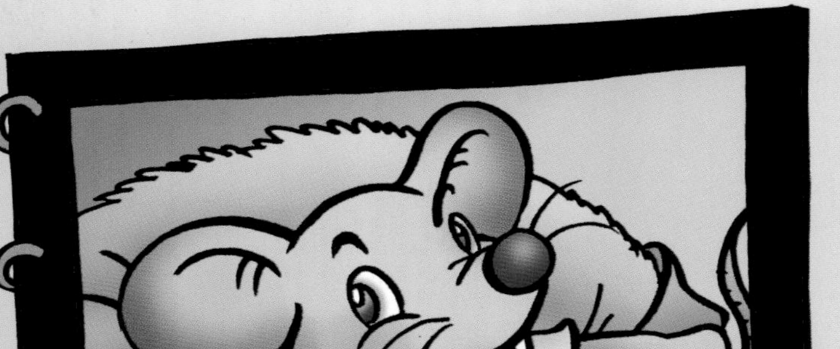

my father

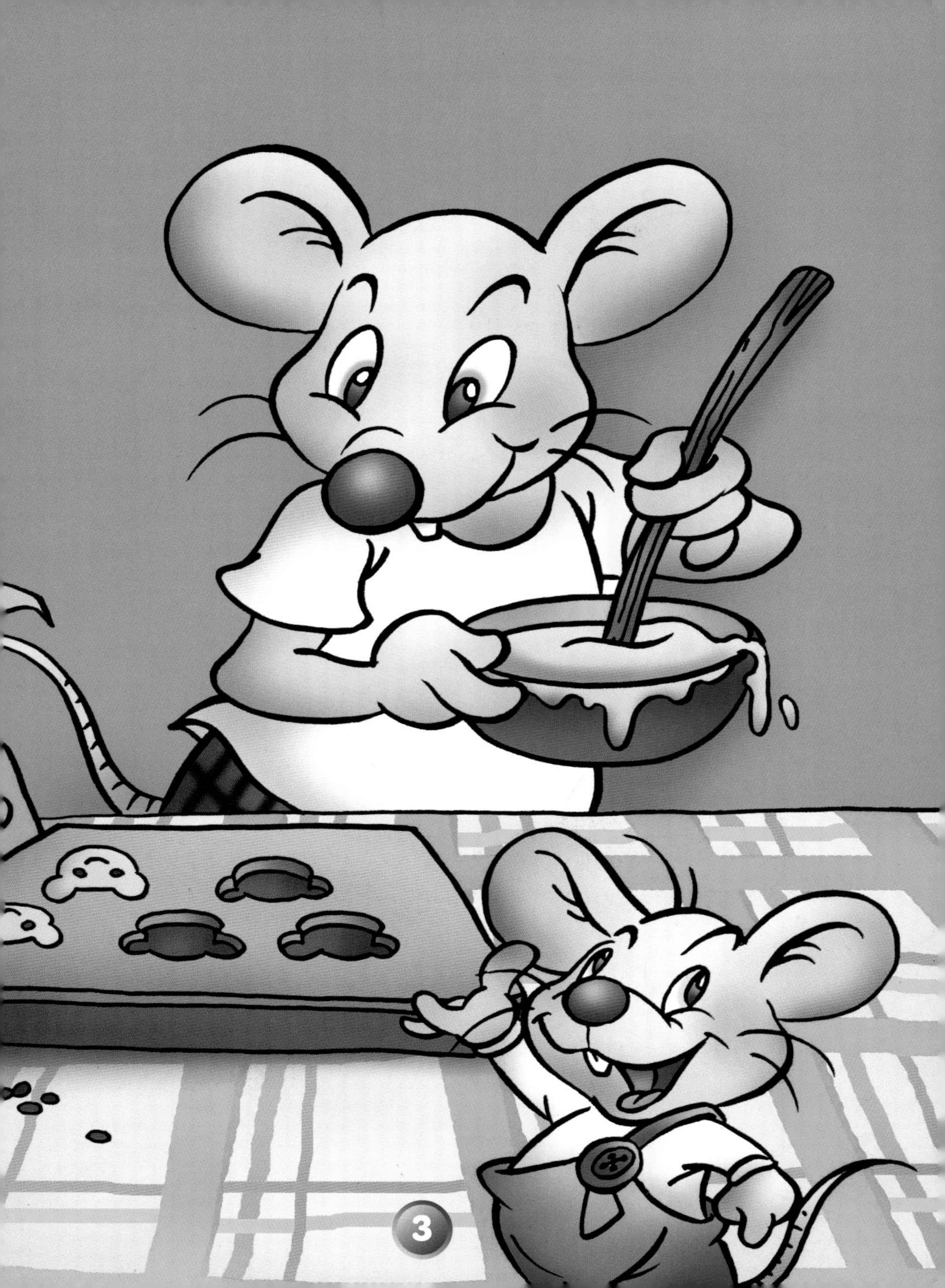

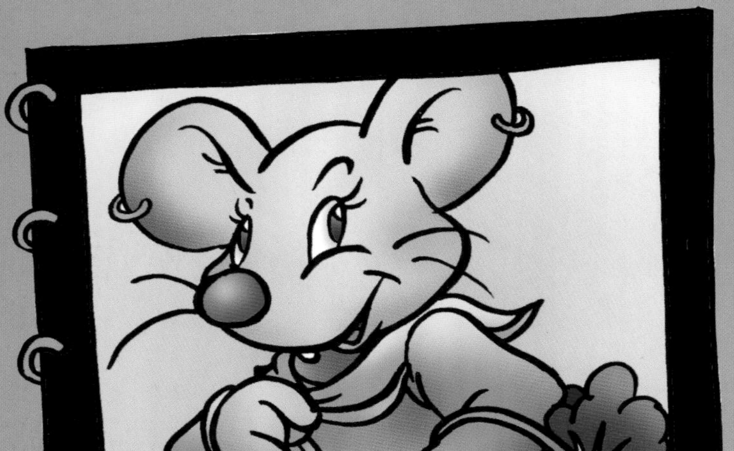

my mother

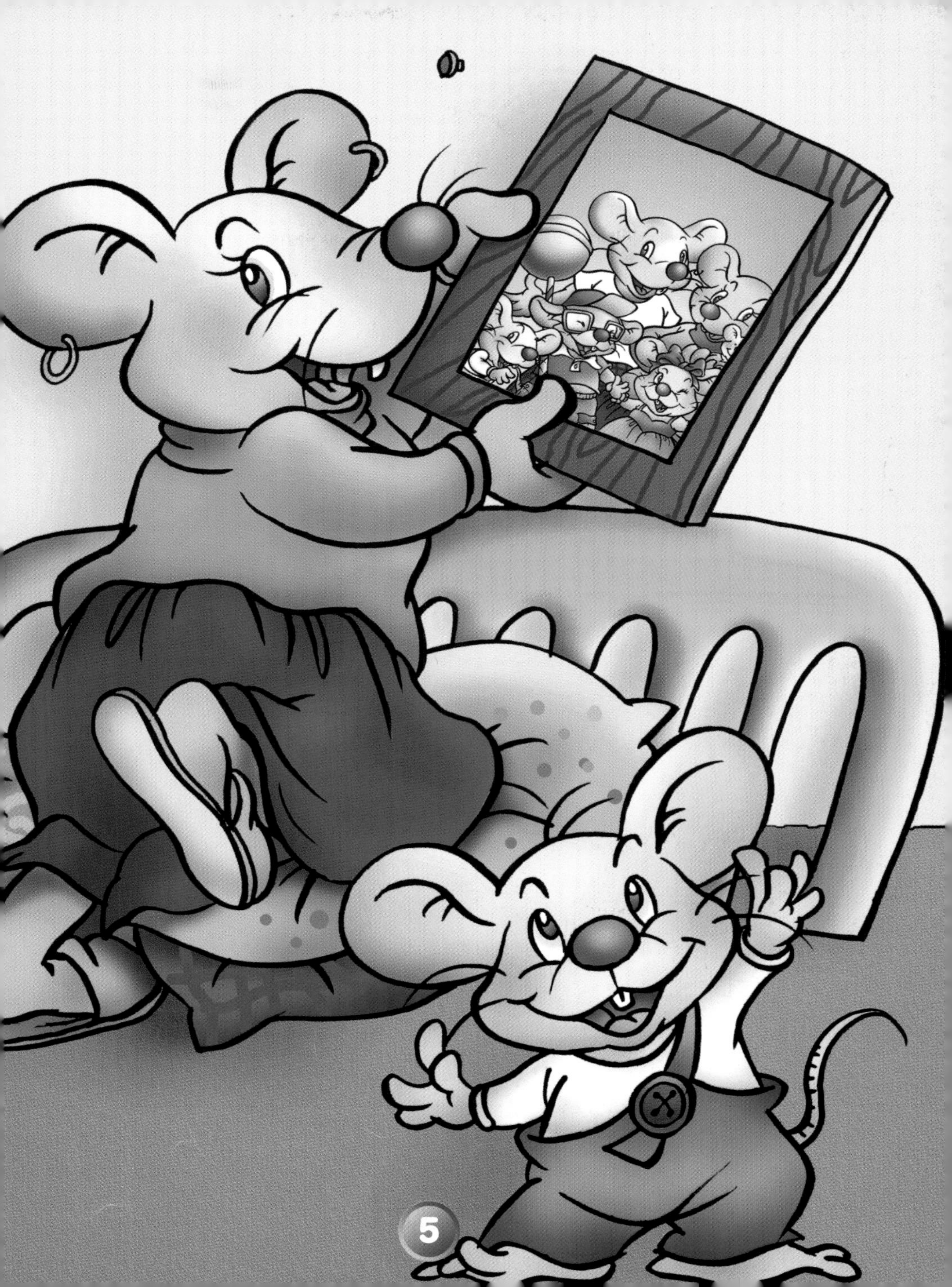

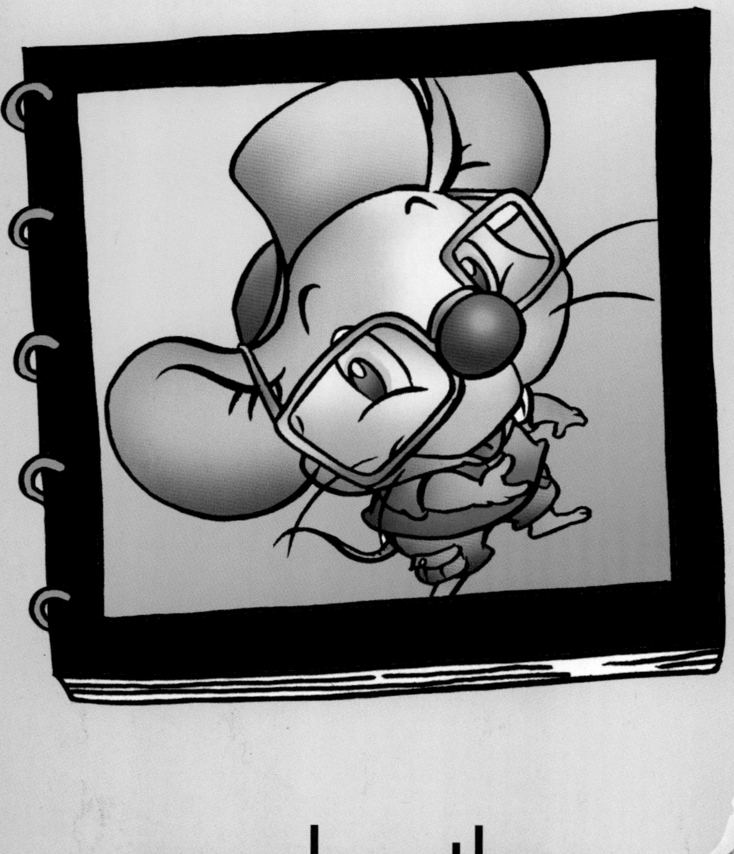

my brother

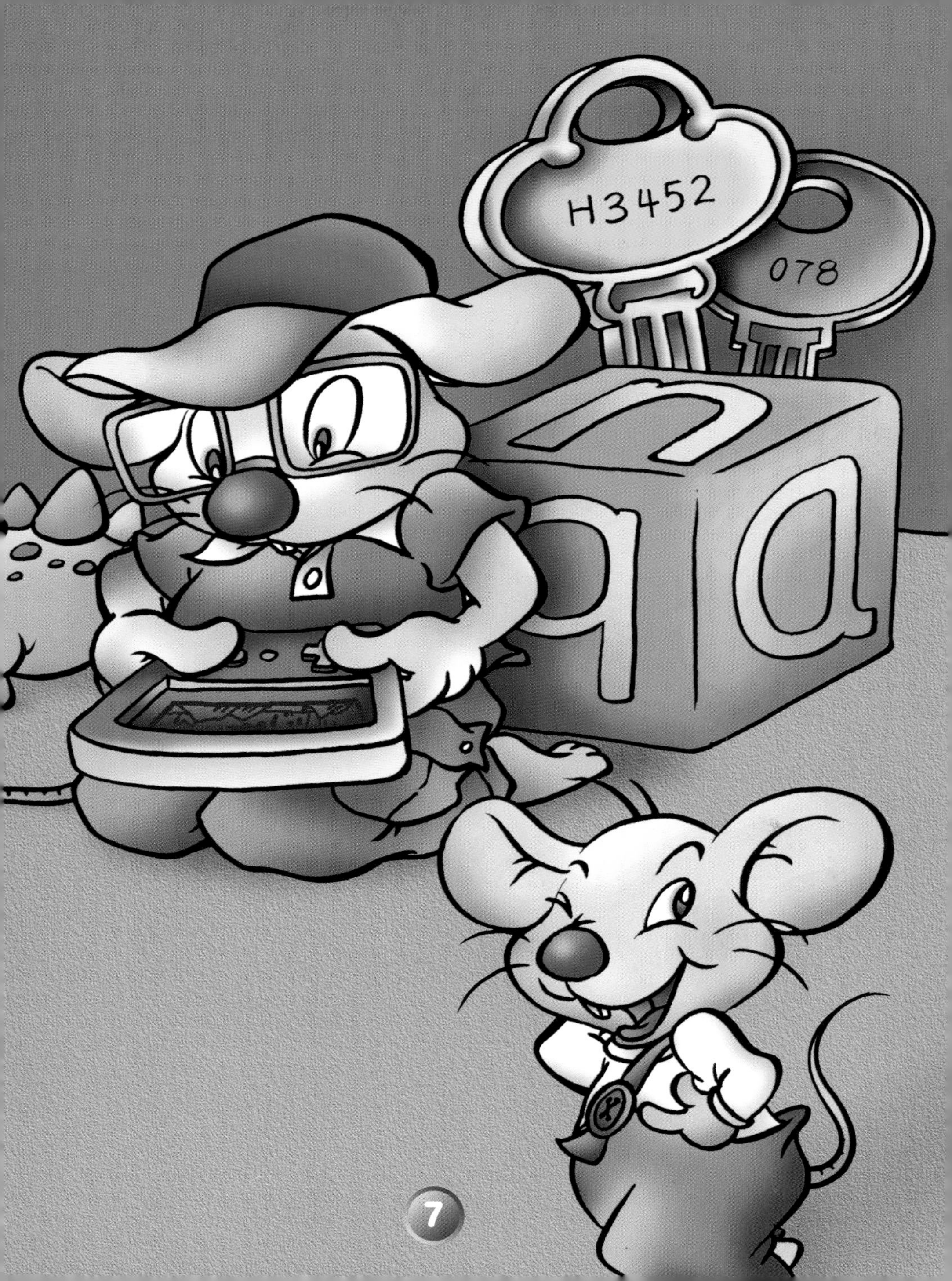
H3452
078

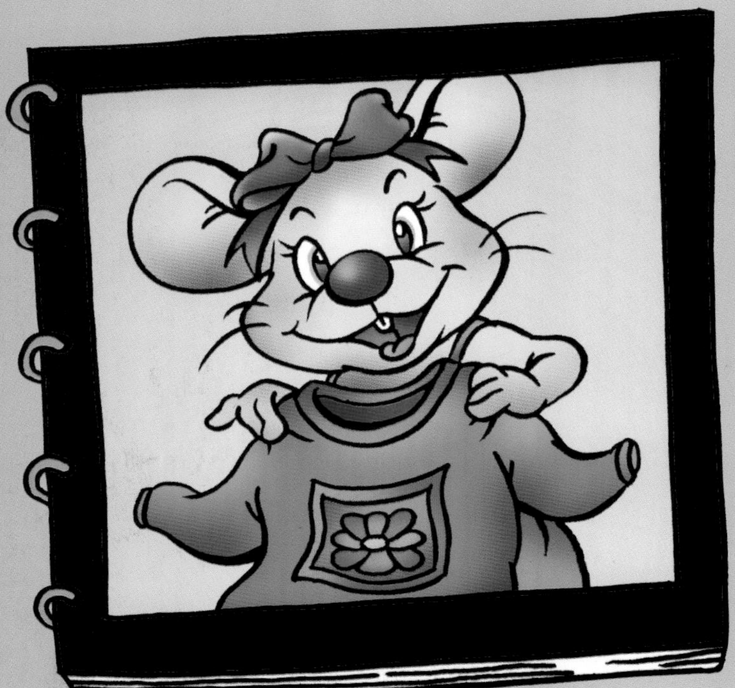

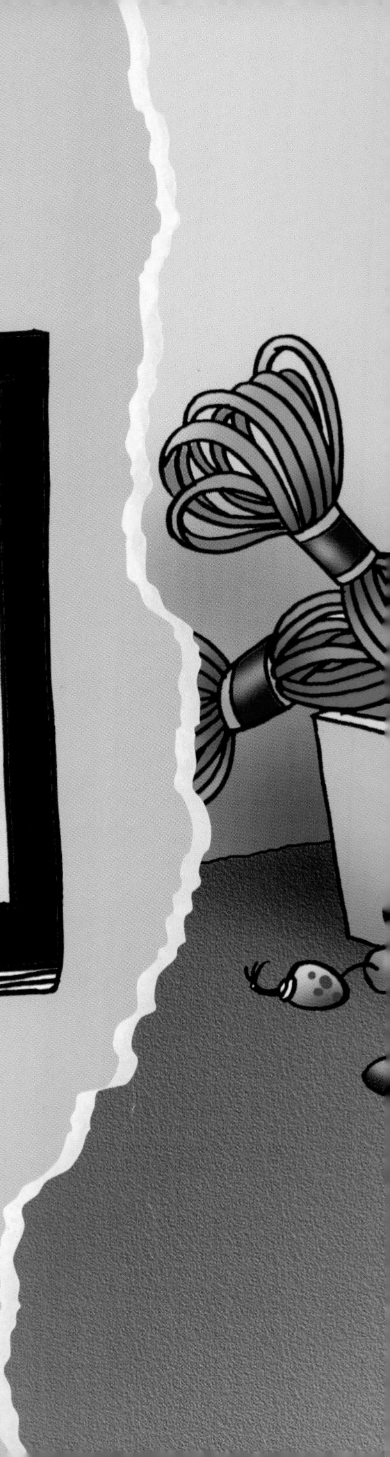

my sister

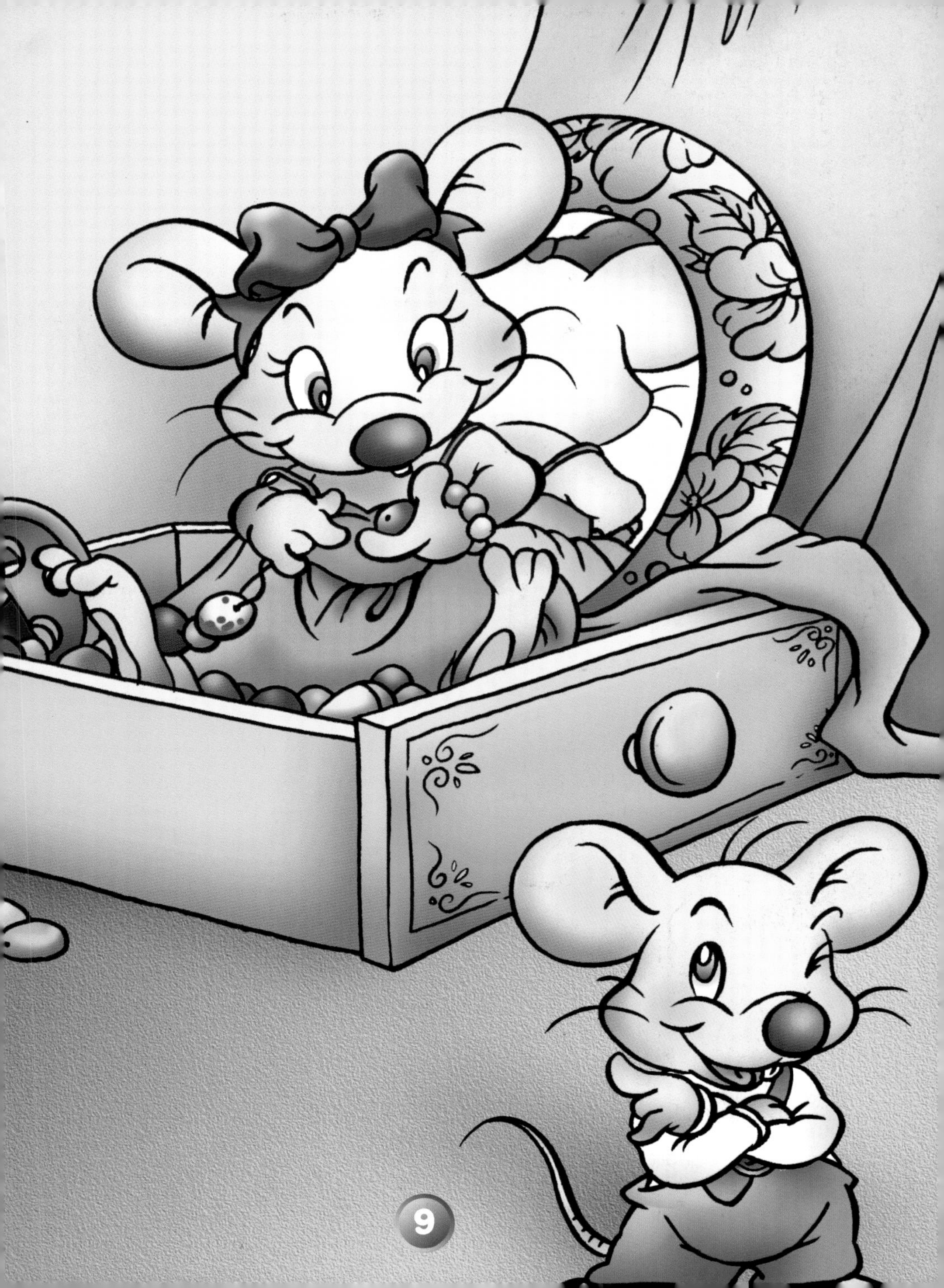

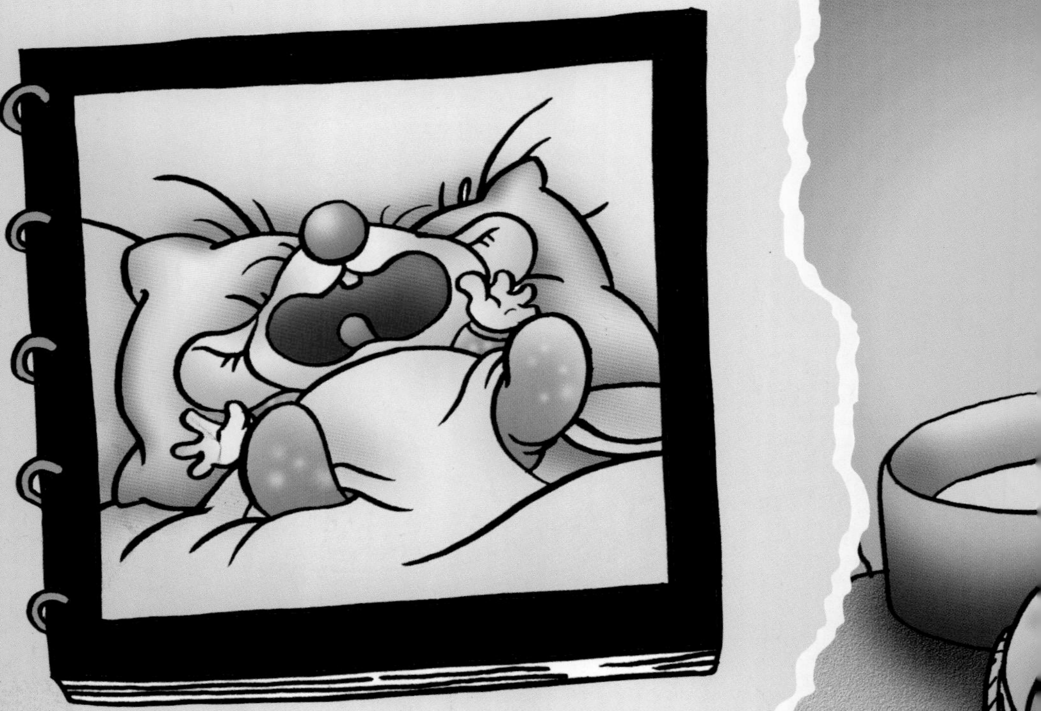

my baby

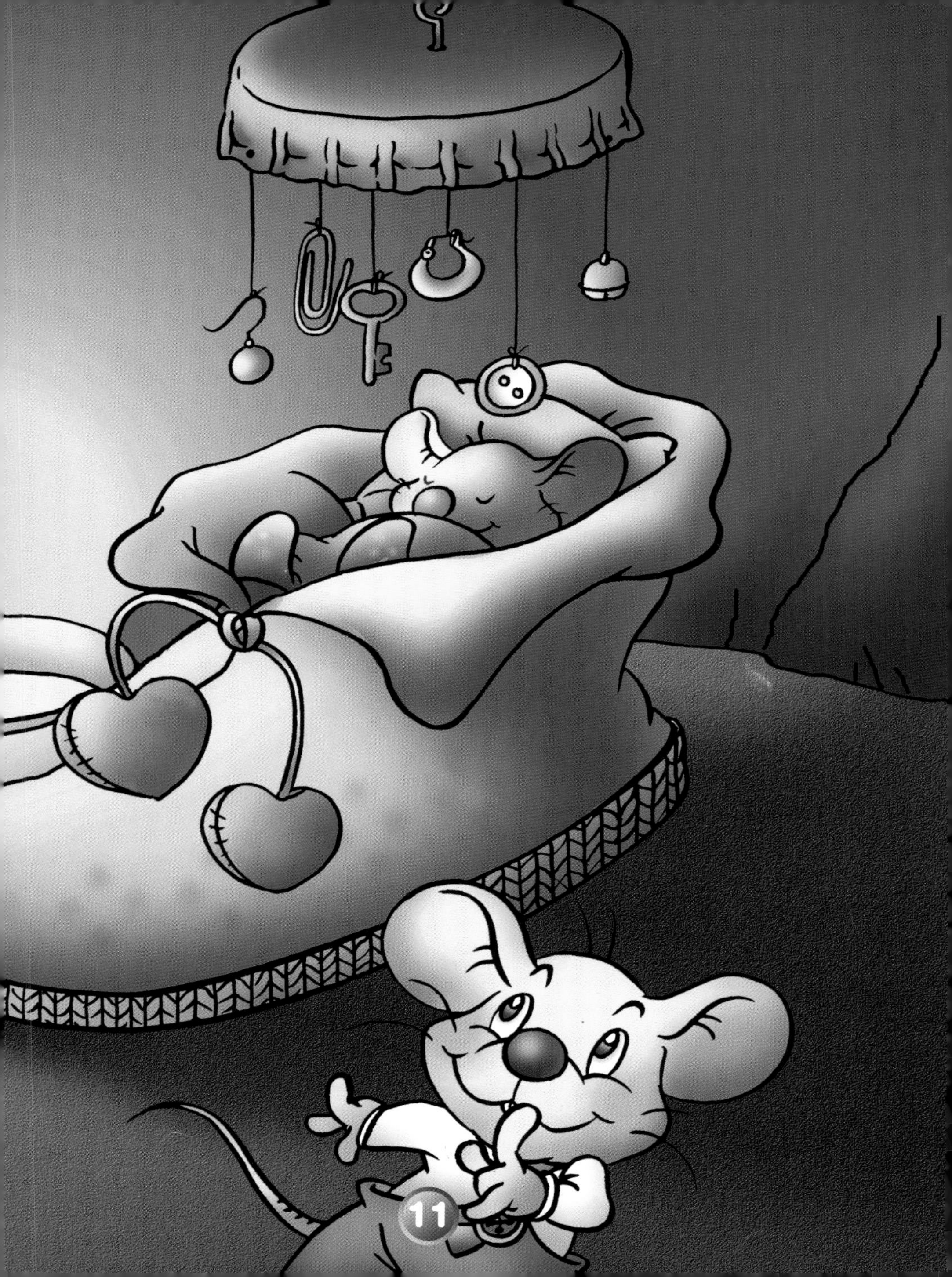

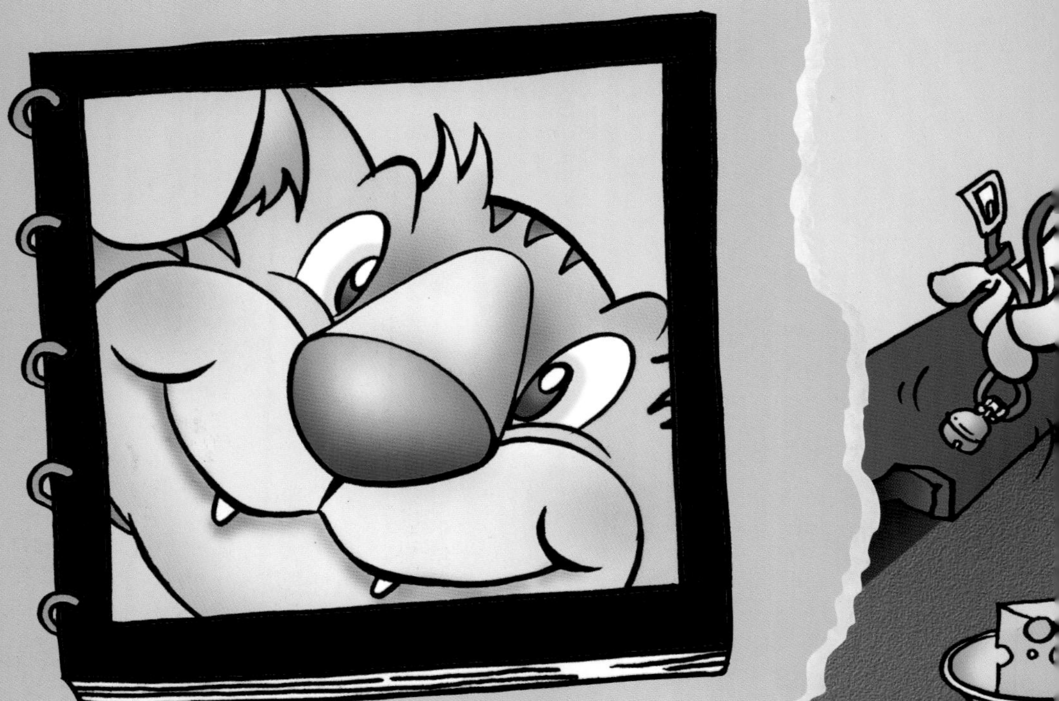

my cat

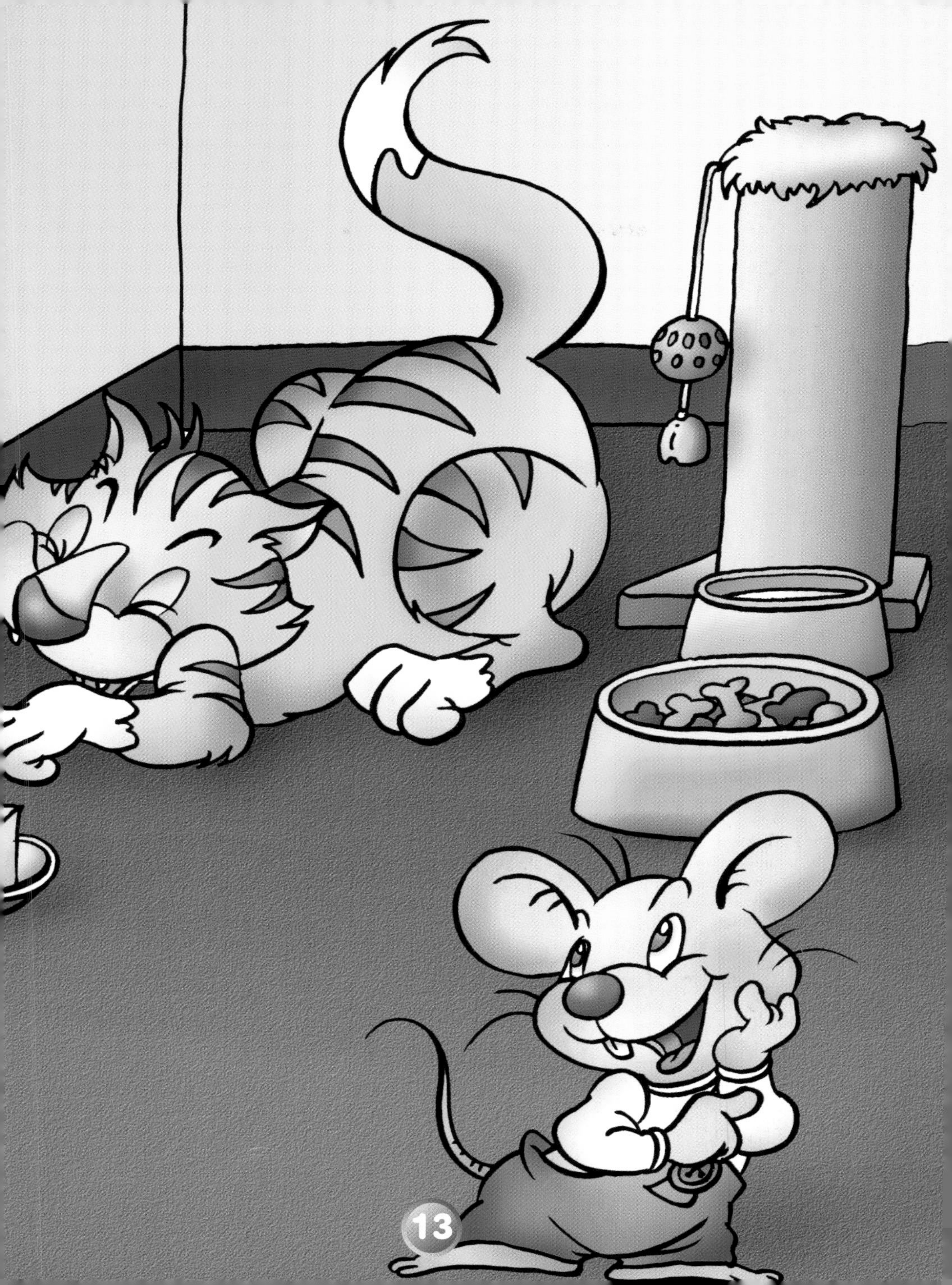

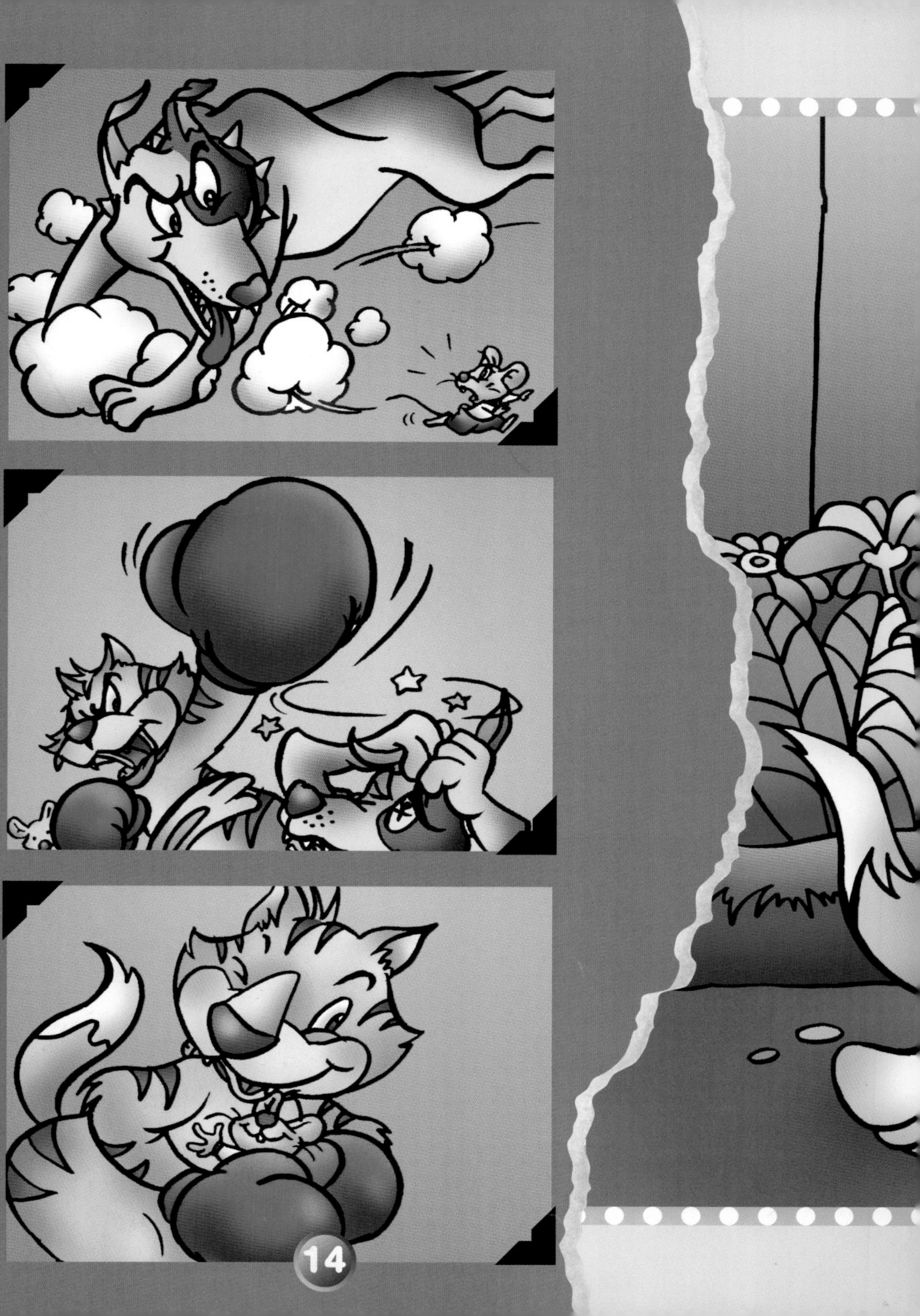

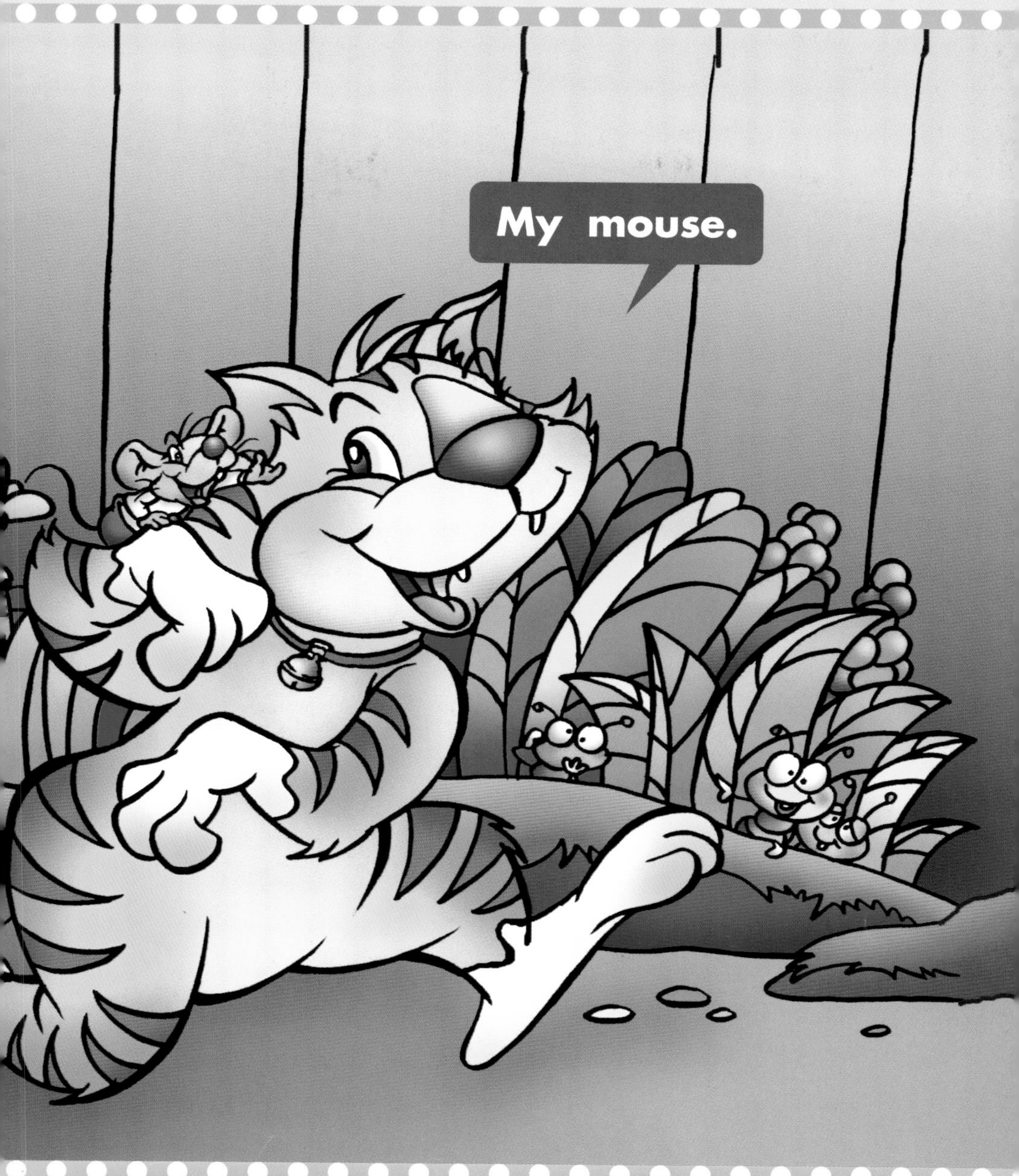
My mouse.

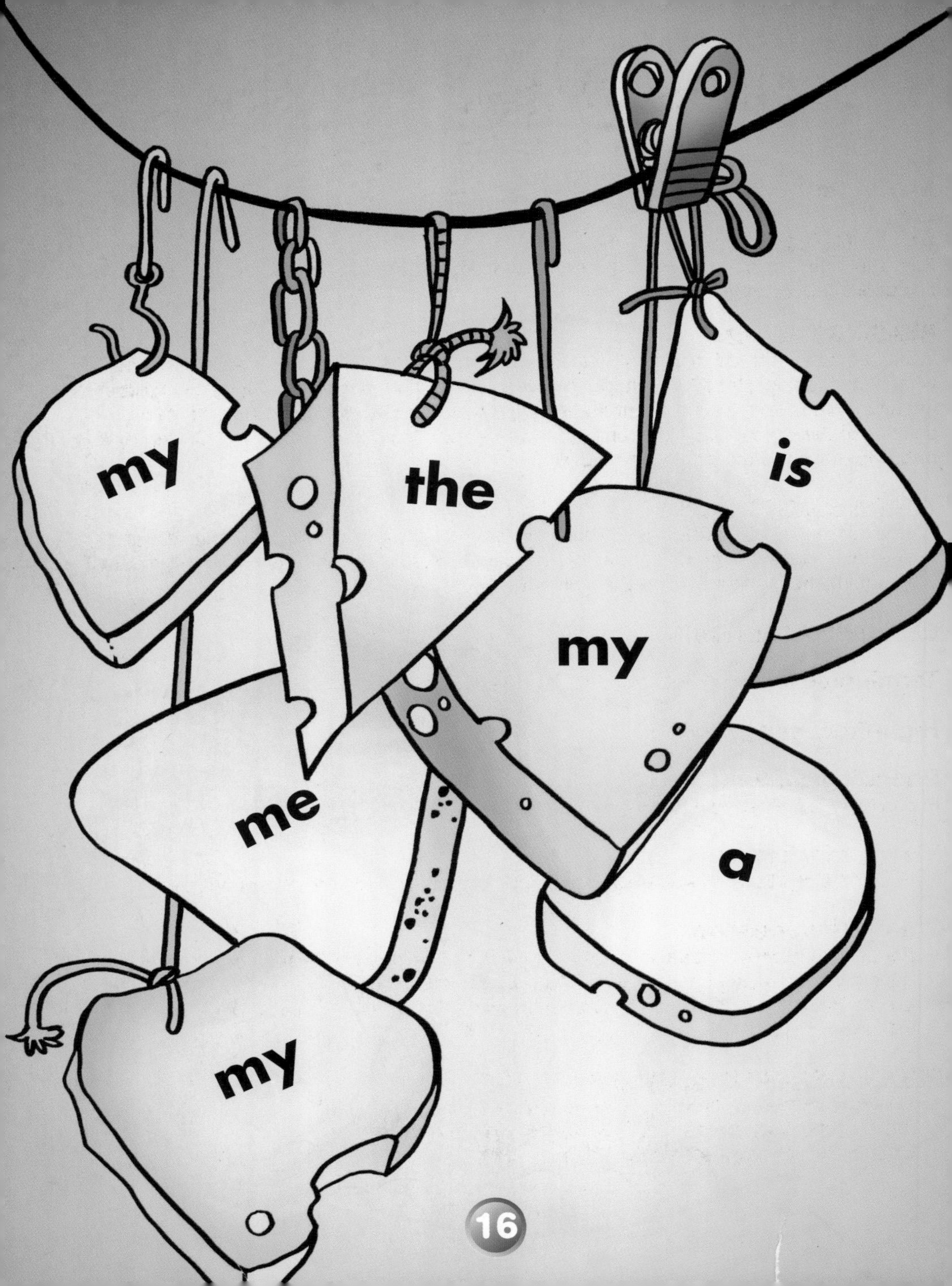
my
the
is
my
me
a
my